✔ **KT-431-397**

Books should be returned or renewed by the last date above. Renew by phone **03000 41 31 31** or online *www.kent.gov.uk/libs*

aries Registration & Archives

C334724442

To Mrs Wood and the children of Upton
St Leonards C of E Primary School.
Keep enjoying your stories! – T. C.

For Olive x – T. N.

STRIPES PUBLISHING LIMITED
An imprint of the Little Tiger Group
1 Coda Studios, 189 Munster Road,
London SW6 6AW

Imported into the EEA by Penguin Random House Ireland,
Morrison Chambers, 32 Nassau Street, Dublin D02 YH68

www.littletiger.co.uk

A paperback original
First published in Great Britain in 2022

Text copyright © Tracey Corderoy, 2022
Illustrations copyright © Tony Neal, 2022

ISBN: 978-1-78895-325-2

Printed and bound in the UK.

MIX
Paper from
responsible sources
FSC® C171272
www.fsc.org

The Forest Stewardship Council® (FSC®) is a global, not-for-profit organization dedicated to
the promotion of responsible forest management worldwide. FSC® defines standards based
on agreed principles for responsible forest stewardship that are supported by environmental,
social, and economic stakeholders. To learn more, visit www.fsc.org

10 8 6 4 2 1 3 5 7 9

THE STORY SHOP

BLAST OFF!

TRACEY CORDEROY
TONY NEAL

LITTLE TIGER
LONDON

WARNING!

Contains aliens, black holes
and super-stinky cheese!

Contents

Welcome to Puddletown High Street!

Looks completely normal, doesn't it?

Normal bakers selling normal bread.

Normal shoe shop selling normal wellies.

Normal toyshop selling normal bats and balls.

But nestled between the hairdresser's and the hardware store (which sells *entirely* normal brooms) is the most **unusual** shop:

The Story Shop sells adventures you can BE in. With real characters you'll *actually* meet!

Shopkeeper Wilbur and his assistant Fred Ferret have props and plots galore.

So, what are you waiting for? Step inside
if you're **BRAVE** enough.

But be warned, *anything might*
happen...

"**Wilbur!**" cried Fred excitedly.
"Are you ready to play Guess Who?"

Fred Ferret loved their daily game
before opening time.

His fluffy little head disappeared into
the props barrel as he flung out the
things he *didn't* want. A wooden knight's
sword, some floppy elephant ears. Even a
squawking cuckoo clock flew past Wilbur's
freshly polished counter.

Wilbur ducked. "**My hat,**" he yelped.

"You nearly knocked the feather clean off!"

"Sorry, Wilbur." Fred's head reappeared from the barrel complete with cowboy hat. "Guess who?"

Wilbur looked up from dusting the till. "Um, Cowboy Jim from the burpy donkey story?"

"*Burpy?*" giggled Fred. "No, here's another clue!"

He peered around their cosy shop with its neat round window and worn wooden floor. Rails of costumes lined the walls alongside shelves crammed with jars of letters. Tucked between the jars were dozens of blank books waiting to be filled with stories.

Behind the counter stood a set of drawers full of story settings and characters. A Jungle drawer teemed with creepy crawlies, while the Ocean one brimmed with bright fish and the Space drawer fizzed with aliens and black holes.

To the side of the counter sat a chest of smaller props. Fred opened the lid and pulled out a bright red bandana. He tied it around his neck, grabbed a clinking money bag, then unhooked a hobby horse from a tall wooden stand.

"Yee haa!"

"Oh, I know!" called Wilbur. "Wild Will Ferret, the meanest outlaw in town?"

"You got it!" laughed Fred, tossing him the money bag. "Well done!"

Fred trotted after Wilbur as he opened the shop door and set the chalkboard outside on the sunny pavement.

"Ahhh," Wilbur smiled. "The perfect day for **an adventure!**"

"Sure is," replied Fred. "And we're ready and waiting."

Back inside, costumes tidied away and props back in the barrel, they'd just started oiling Sir Squeakalot the knight when **ting! ting!** went the brass bell above the door.

"First customer!" cheered Fred. "But who will it be? A grouchy granny? A bonkers bear? A crusty old—" He stopped as a small mouse marched through the door. "Oh."

"Oh?" scowled the mouse. "Oh! *Really?* Is OH all you can say?"

"I'm s-so sorry," began Fred. "I—"

"Typical!" Mouse tutted. "Disappointed I'm not a *bear*. Well, *let me tell* you, I'm as brave as one. And don't get me started on *skilled*. Why, I can balance a chair ... on my chin ... while tightrope walking ... across a swamp! *AND* fit seventy-three marshmallows in my cheeks all at once."

Fred and Wilbur exchanged glances. What a boasty little fellow!

"So, sir, what can we do for you?" asked Wilbur.

"Isn't that obvious?" replied the mouse. "I want an adventure. **A story adventure.** Isn't that what your shop *sells*?"

Suddenly two drawers behind the counter wriggled open. Any mention of a new story and the characters inside were all ears!

Mouse's eyes widened as an octopus's tentacle flopped out of one and a snake slithered out of the other. Fred dashed to pop them away.

"ESCAPED character ALERT!"

"Keen beans, Olivia and Stanley!" grinned Wilbur. "Though not right for your story, Mouse." Wilbur prided himself on finding the right story for every customer.

"Let's get started, shall we?" Making a quick list, Wilbur wandered around the shop gathering bits Mouse could 'try for size'...

"Perhaps a brush with a **brontosaurus?**," pondered Wilbur.

"Or a **thrilling whodunnit?**"

"Or a **fairy tale!**"

"No, no!" Mouse dumped the curls at once. "I want something *awesome* – *amazing* – *incredible*. **Something out of this world.**"

"Out of this world..." Wilbur twiddled his moustache. "Of course!"

He grabbed two shiny silver costumes off a rail, handed one to Fred and swept Mouse into the changing room. When he came back out...

"I'm a **Space Mouse!**" he cried.

"And I'm a **Space Ferret**," Fred exclaimed, popping up from behind the counter.

Mouse glowered. "Wait – you're coming? I don't need a babysitter!"

"Fred always goes with the customer," said Wilbur. "On every adventure..."

No sooner had he said the word 'adventure' than a blank book on the shelf gave a little jiggle as if itching to get the story started.

"Right then!" Wilbur whisked the feather from his hat and waved it over a patch of bare floorboards. They parted with a swish! and up rose a large cooking pot full to the brim with a shimmering inky-blue liquid. Hooked over the rim was a big silver spoon.

"This is the **Story Pot,**" Wilbur told Mouse as Fred fished out an alien from the Space drawer. He was small and green and clutching a jar filled with a gooey yellow liquid. He dived into the pot with a snorty little giggle.

Next they added the jiggling book and a sprinkle of letters from a jar.

"Letters?" shrugged Mouse.

"All stories need **words...**" said Fred.

Wilbur spooned in an assortment of story props – twinkling stars, dice, screwdrivers and *lots* of stinky cheese. Then he handed Fred three objects to put in his backpack.

"Emergency items," Fred told Mouse. "To get us out of tricky situations."

"Biscuits?" Mouse frowned. "A toy shield? **Party poppers!** No lasers? No moon buggies? No—"

"Just stir it," Wilbur said with a wink. "And remember, Mouse, your story is what *you* make it."

"Yeah, yeah!" As Mouse started to stir, Wilbur passed Fred a small toy rocket, which he slipped into his pocket.

"All set then!" Fred cried, holding the spoon too, and...

WHOOSH! an inky jet of bubbles flew from the pot. They splashed off shelves, ricocheted off costumes and plipped and plopped off props.

Then suddenly...

POP! the bubbles vanished. And Mouse and Fred were gone.

"What on EARTH...?" cried Mouse.

"Not *Earth*," grinned Fred. "Stars and craters! Look – we're on the Moon."

"Of course, I *knew* that," muttered Mouse, "as I'm BRILLIANT at spotting things."

"Like those *houses*?" Fred pointed.

"Eh?" Mouse looked. They were yellow and wedge-shaped, with holes.

"Poo! They don't half pong," said Fred.

"I *like* it," replied Mouse, his nose twitching. "And if I'm not mistaken..." He marched towards one.

"Don't touch anything!" Fred warned. "Not until we've sussed the place out."

"My adventure, my rules – Wilbur said so!" called Mouse.

He stopped at a house, sniffed again, then took a big bite out of a windowsill.

"Mmmm, *cheese*," said Mouse, licking his whiskers. "Just as I suspected as I'm BRILLIANT at—"

An alarm shrieked out and a gooey yellow liquid exploded from a nearby crater. Fred dived for cover behind a neat cheese hedge but Mouse was too slow.

OO!
OOO!

"*Slime*," he tutted, shaking off the
splatters as he ducked down beside Fred.
"Honestly! What NINNIES would
booby-trap their houses?"

"*Shh…*" Fred nudged him.

"Don't nudge me, this is my—"

"*Shh – look!*"

A swarm of small, green one-eyed aliens
were racing from their houses towards them.

They looked like peas, and each had one eye on a stalk, like a periscope. Fred saw the giggly alien who had dived into the Story Pot, except he wasn't smiling now. He was glowering and muttering crossly, "Nibble-nibble!"

"What's the matter?" huffed Mouse as the aliens circled them. "I only had a *teeny* nibble!"

Suddenly a **WHOOSHING** sound above made them all look up. A bubble-shaped pod was flying in through the darkness, a whirring propeller at its base. Through its gleaming domed window Fred and Mouse saw a much BIGGER alien...

He had a triangular-shaped body covered in mouldy blue patches. He reminded Mouse of a lump of Gorgonzola cheese! His mouth was big and grumpy. And his eyes (he had two) were frowning.

Fred also counted two pairs of arms. One pair were small and inside the pod. The other pair dangled outside and were super long – *with pincers*.

At once, the little aliens all bowed their one eye and bobbed wobbly curtsies. "This must be their leader," said Fred.

"I knew that!" muttered Mouse.

As the pod came in to land, two skinny legs with chicken feet zooped out of its base. The moment they touched the ground, the leader marched straight over to Mouse.

"How DARE you eat our houses

– **again!**" he roared in a weird tinny voice.

"Well – how DARE you ROAR at ME!" roared Mouse. "That's rude!"

The little aliens gasped at Mouse's cheek. Their leader looked fit to

explode!

Fred quickly stepped in front of Mouse. "Pleased to meet you, Mr ... um ... Alien," he said. "I'm Fred, and you are?"

"Gordon!" snapped the leader. "Gordon Zola."

"I *knew* it!" cried Mouse. "Like Gorgonzola – that stinky cheese!"

The leader glowered at Mouse. "*Last time* you ate a whole front door, and *now* you return to eat a windowsill! We thought you'd LEARNED YOUR LESSON – but clearly your punishment wasn't hard enough. You—"

"Hang on," chipped in Fred. "He's been here before?"

"Affirmative!" Gordon Zola nodded. "The Big Cheese invaded us last month."

He eyed Mouse closely. "Or is it HE? For *this* one's ears look somewhat smaller...?"

"How DARE you!" cried Mouse. "My ears are enormous and I'm *totally* the Big Cheese, thank you!"

Fred pulled him aside. "Why did you say that? You'll get us into big troub—"

"*Stop spoiling my story*," hissed Mouse. "I choose what happens and this Big Cheese guy sounds AWESOME."

Mouse turned back to Gordon Zola.

"Right! I AM the Big Cheese. So, what are you going to do about it?"

"One more nibble and you will be ERASED," cried the leader. And from one of his pincers zooped a pencil *with a rubber on.*

"Erased? O-outrageous!" spluttered Mouse. "You can't rub me out of my OWN story!"

"We'll see about that," Gordon Zola replied. "But first it's time to teach you another lesson."

He clicked his pincers and suddenly –
"Oi!"

Mouse had been scooped up by his tail, and several aliens were carting him off.

"Put me down!" he yelled.

Fred hurried after Mouse, trying to calm him down. But Mouse was having none of it. "I **demand,**" Mouse roared, helplessly batting the air, "to know where you're *taking* me. You ... NINNIES!"

After an uncomfortable ride, Mouse was plonked down in Gordon Zola's enormous garden.

Everything was made of cheese.

Cheese flowers, cheese trees, a cheese telescope ... there were even cheese statues.

"All of Gordon Zola!" gasped Fred.

"You'll remember – *Big Cheese*," Gordon said to Mouse, "that your punishment last time (as you *insisted* you were STRONG) was to lift my statues into position."

"Sure," lied Mouse. "And carrying them was EASY too!"

Fred rolled his eyes.

"In *that* case," snapped Gordon, jabbing his pencil at Mouse, "today you'll prove your strength even more."

"Bring it on!" cried Mouse, flexing his tiny muscles. "The Big Cheese can do ANYTHING."

"*Stop boasting or you'll be erased,*" whispered Fred.

"As if!" Mouse puffed out his chest.

"Just do as he says, while I look for an escape," said Fred as the aliens scrabbled for the best spots to watch the action!

"Right," said the leader, pointing all four arms to a big pile of cheese boulders. "Make me a Moon House out of those. Somewhere I can sit and watch the stars."

Mouse rolled up his sleeves. "Easy-peasy!" Except the boulders were heavier than he thought.

Much heavier!

As Mouse huffed and puffed, Fred took a sneaky peek through Gordon's telescope, searching for a way out. But he couldn't spy any black holes or shooting stars…

"**Done!**" yelled Mouse finally, his cheeks bright pink and his ears dangling down to his space boots.

Gordon inspected his new Moon House, boulder by boulder.

"Hmmm, I suppose it will do."

"Only DO?" shrieked Mouse. "What's WRONG with it? Too low? Oh, sorry I didn't stick it up a tree!"

"H-he didn't mean it!"
spluttered Fred, but...

"Good idea!" Gordon nodded.
"And while you're at it, why not put my
throne in it too?"

Mouse glared at Gordon.

"No fuss," mouthed Fred.

"Grrr!" rumbled Mouse. "FINE!"

Mouse muttered and moaned and grunted
and groaned as, boulder by boulder, he
carted the Moon House up a ladder into
a tree!

While he did that, Fred 'took a stroll'
but he was really checking the garden
for escape holes.

"Done!" yelled Mouse *again*,
dumping in the throne and
stomping down the ladder
to Gordon.

"So what NEXT?" shrieked Mouse.
"Eh? Come on! Why not fire me up there –
from a **cannon?**"

Fred froze. How was *this* not making
a *fuss...*?

"H-he didn't mean—" Fred called
over. But out squeaked
a cannon – and...

BOOM!

Mouse flew across the lawn and landed in a heap in front of Gordon Zola.

As the little aliens clapped, Fred crossed the lawn to help, when – "Whoa!" – he almost fell down *a crater*.

It was small and buried deep beneath a patch of whiffy ferns. But jump down *there* and they could tunnel away!

Fred raced over to tell Mouse. But Mouse was too busy fuming!

"You ... ALIENS," he thundered, getting to his feet and straightening his helmet.

"Never *satisfied*. I bet you'll want a present next?"

"Affirmative!" nodded Gordon.

"I— What?" Mouse stopped. "You want ... a p-present?"

Mouse looked at Fred, whose eyes grew wide.

"Oh, Mouse," whispered Fred. "What have you done now? We don't have a present!"

But suddenly he remembered the biscuits in his backpack.

He whipped them out and turned to Gordon with a bow.

"Your present, oh, great leader!" Fred twinkled. "A wondrous Earth delicacy! And especially yummy ... *with cheese.*"

Gordon smiled. Fred smiled. Mouse, though, did not.

"But those biscuits are *plain* ones," Mouse tutted. "How boring! Now, *I* could make them into a MAGNIFICENT cheesecake if you've got some spare cream cheese?"

Fred gaped. If Mouse had *only* stopped boasting, they could have made their escape.

"Do it!" commanded Gordon. "But it had better BE magnificent, or else..." He waved the pencil under Mouse's nose.

"It's bye-bye *forever* – Big Cheese!"

Mouse and Fred were shown to a shiny kitchen inside a gigantic crater.

It had a gleaming domed roof, a larder (full of cheese) and a big, snazzy lime-green cooker.

Aliens from everywhere were on their way to watch. Not *only* had the Big Cheese been punished (again), but he'd promised them a magnificent cheesecake. They were even going to *film* it for the intergalactic cooking show *Moon Munches*.

While Mouse checked out the larder, Fred searched for *another* escape route, peering under cupboards and poking behind the cooker.

At first, he found nothing. But as he was checking beside the sink, he happened upon a rubbish chute in the shape of a biggish black hole.

"**Bingo!**" beamed Fred. This was it! Their way out.

"Psst – Mouse!" he called over. But it was too late. With a sudden...

BANG!

the kitchen door burst open and swarms of excited little aliens pattered in, eager for the show to begin. Gordon Zola took his seat at the front.

"Roll the camera!"

As Mouse and Fred threw on their aprons...

"Psst, *Mouse*," whispered Fred. "I just saw an es—"

"**Ferret,** kindly be quiet," tutted Mouse. "*I'm* head chef and *you'll* only speak – or help – *if* I ask. And that's NOT because I cannot do it by myself. I'm just kind."

"*But ... but,*" gabbled Fred. "*I just saw an escape route!*"

Mouse shrugged. "Escaping will have to wait. I'm on telly!"

He marched to the counter and an alien snapped a clapperboard.

"Nibble!" he called.

"Eh?" Mouse shrugged.

"I think that means 'Action!'" whispered Fred.

Fred could see Gordon, just a whisker away, pencil at the ready if Mouse messed up.

Mouse gazed down at his ingredients. "So ... hmmm..."

"You do know *how* to make a cheesecake?" whispered Fred.

"I ... *pfff* ... how hard can it *be*?" Mouse replied. "Besides, like I said, I *might* let *you* help. Just a little."

"Right, aliens," said Mouse, beaming at the audience. "Prepare to be amazed at, well – me!"

Then he weighed (with Fred's help), whisked (with Fred's help), spooned (with Fred's help), baked (with Fred's help). And finally, his **MAGNIFICENT** cheesecake was...

Everyone tucked in – "Nibble-nibble!" –
until the cheesecake was all gone.

"See? I'm a genius!" nodded Mouse.

Gordon looked thoughtful. "Yes, cooking
does seem to be the ONE thing you're good
at," he said. "And we need a new chef, so
you must stay – FOREVER. Your washer-
upper too."

"Who m-me?" spluttered Fred. "No –
we c-couldn't."

"But that is an ORDER!" barked
Gordon. And from one of his pincers zooped
a padlock to chain them to the kitchen sink!

"Time to go!" gulped Fred.

"Affirmative!" nodded Mouse.

"Black hole – beside the sink!" yelled
Fred.

And, waving goodbye, they took it
at speed...

Winner Winner!

DONK!

The black hole dumped Fred and Mouse in a big, colourful ball pit.

Fred looked around and his eyes lit up. "Snap, roller skates ... hopscotch!" he cried. "I think we've landed on a *Planet of Games.*"

"*Well now* – I'm *aces* at games," boasted Mouse, juggling a handful of balls. "Ludo, tiddlywinks, hide-and-seek... And don't get me STARTED on tag."

He gave Fred a nudge. "Why, I could even juggle **ALL** of these balls in one paw ... if I wanted to!"

"I'm sure you could, Mouse," chuckled Fred, scrambling out of the pit.

"Hey! Wait for me!" cried Mouse, disappearing under the sea of balls.

Fred leaned in and pulled him out.

"I could have managed," huffed Mouse, straightening his helmet. "Come on, let's explore!"

"The aliens who live here must be FUN," said Fred as he strolled after Mouse.

There were bats and balls. There were frisbees and skipping ropes. There was a huge, ride-on chess set, and board games galore.

There was even a giant snakes and ladders game going up one of the walls.

"**Cool**," said Fred. "You climb **real** ladders. But where are all the snakes?"

Mouse shrugged. "Look at **that**," he cried, pointing out a *jigsaw-puzzle* sky. "And – oh boy!"

In the distance was a funfair with a massive roller coaster.

"Race you there!" laughed Mouse.

"No, *wait*," cried Fred. Something wasn't right. The place looked completely deserted. "Mouse, where are the *aliens* who live here?"

They peered around...

"That *balloon!*" gasped Mouse, pointing at a curious maze made of candy floss. "It just moved!"

They hurried over. Floating up from inside the maze were three balloons on strings.

"The green one moved," Mouse insisted. "And the purple one's moving *now.*"

"*So is the* *red* one!" whispered Fred. "Maybe the *aliens* are holding the strings. Let's investigate – but quietly."

They tiptoed in.

"Follow me," said Mouse. "I'm BRILLIANT at mazes. Right! Left."

He marched off and Fred followed.

"I meant RIGHT," grumbled Mouse. But Fred had spotted something...

"There!"

Just a hedge away, the three balloons had gathered in a bunch. Then Fred and Mouse heard voices...

"Red wins!" chuckled one. "I reached the middle first."

"Well done, Captain Bushy!" cried another voice.

Following the voices, Fred and Mouse peeped around the hedge ... and gasped.

What weird little creatures the aliens were!

"They're just *whiskers*," said Fred. "How are they holding the balloons?"

"Oi! Aliens!" blurted Mouse, leaping into view. "Where's the rest of you?"

FWITT!

The whiskers all huddled together quivering.

"We didn't mean to scare you," said Fred. "We've just—"

"Don't tell!" squeaked the littlest wispy bunch.

"Please and thank you," added the curly whiskers politely.

"Best leave..." said the bushy bunch, his voice low and wise.

"Before she—"

"Wait – *leave?*" interrupted Mouse. "Ridiculous! We only just *got* here."

"*Mouse,*" whispered Fred. "I think they're trying to *tell* us something."

Fred stepped a little closer. "So, who's this '*she*'?"

But suddenly... **BOOM!** a huge dice bowled in, squashing the hedges flat. The whiskers dived for cover, along with Fred and Mouse.

The dice came to a halt in front of them. A door in one of the dots then opened – and out 'she' came...

The powerful droid was made from shimmering metal. Her face was pointy, her eyes were mean and she wore a helmet with very sharp horns. Her tummy, though, looked like a gumball machine – see-through and full of jelly beans!

"*Visitors!*" smiled the droid. "I never have visitors. In fact, the last I had were ... *them.*"

She glared at the whiskers. "How DARE you touch my STUFF without asking!"

And lowering her horns...

BANG!

BANG!

BANG!

went their balloons.

She turned back to Fred and Mouse. "I'm Phoebe Fairplay. I live on Planet Winner next door. But *this* is my Games Zone."

"I love games," piped up Mouse. "I'm aces at them too."

"Well, let's hope you're better than them." Phoebe waved a hand at the whiskers.

"Who...?" began Fred. "I mean, why—"

"Are they just whiskers? A very good question!" Phoebe smiled. "When their rocket crash-landed here they had bodies too. I challenged them to a game of snap. And when they lost..."

She stroked her helmet's *left* horn.

"...I vanished them! I call them the Barely Theres!" she went on. "They've been here for years. I was kind enough to let them keep their whiskers, but to get their *bodies* back..."

Her *right* horn flashed purple.

"...They need to beat me. But they never do!"

Fred gave Mouse a warning nudge. "Well, it's lovely to meet you but we'd better be off."

"Are you CRAZY?" cried Mouse. "I want to play. I could beat *her* any day."

"You think so?" smirked Phoebe. "Here we play for jelly beans. *If* you win, you get ALL the flavours."

"And if you l-lose?" Fred gulped, and Phoebe's eyes lit up.

"You'll see!"

"I challenge you to a game of tiddlywonks!" cried Phoebe.

"I accept!" Mouse nodded. "Except – silly you! I think you mean tiddlywinks?"

"No – wonks." Phoebe smiled. She whistled loudly and from a nearby cave out thumped two creatures. They were covered in hair and looked like giant robotic fleas.

"These are wonks," said Phoebe, striding over to a large pitch made of sparkly space dust. "The rules are simple. We each ride a wonk and have a pile of tiddlys we flick through hoops."

The tiddlys looked like frisbees and the hoops like giant bubble blowers.

"The winner," smiled Phoebe, climbing on to her wonk, "will be the one who flicks all their tiddlys through their hoop first."

"Easy-peasy!" boasted Mouse. He beckoned to Fred to help him on to his wonk.

"I've got a bad feeling about this," said Fred as he gave Mouse a leg up.

"You worry too much," huffed Mouse as the wonk tossed its head angrily, almost throwing him off. "I can beat her with my eyes closed."

"I think it's best if you keep them open!" gulped Fred.

Fred watched from the sidelines with
the Barely Theres who looked very twitchy
indeed. And very soon Fred saw why. Out
on to the pitch thumped a whole **herd**
of wonks that looked like they meant
trouble.

"And these are the Boofers!" Phoebe announced.

"W-what do…" began Fred. But Phoebe raised a hand.

"You'll see!"

PEEP!

She blew a whistle and the game began. Well, it did for *HER.*

"**Move!**" bellowed Mouse. But his wonk was going nowhere with the Boofers boofing them back.

"Phoebe's cheating!" yelled Mouse. "They're only tackling **me.**"

BOOF!

Mouse was right. The Boofers were leaving Phoebe alone, so the way to her hoop was clear.

Her wonk was fast too, and...

DING! DING! DING!

Phoebe's tiddlys were soaring through *her* hoop! In no time at all she'd flicked them all.

"Ha! I win!" she cried.

Her prize was a golden goblet of jelly beans. She gulped them down in one.

"You cheat!" roared Mouse as he and Fred marched up to see the sweets tumble into her tummy.

"Am not!" cried Phoebe. "Anyway," she said. "Now you get the *Loser's Prize.*"

"I— What...?" Mouse stopped. "I ... get a *prize?*" At this the Barely Theres whimpered.

"I don't think it's the sort of prize you want," whispered Fred.

"Don't be silly!" huffed Mouse. "A prize is a prize. I want it – now!"

Phoebe nodded.

"Then kindly turn round," she said.

Mouse spun round. And as he did, the *left* horn on Phoebe's helmet began to glow. Silently it swivelled to and fro, searching out its target, and –

WHOOOO

A great gush of orange powder shot out of the tip, hitting Mouse square on the tail.

"It tickles!" he giggled. "It's so—"

But suddenly he stopped and his bright smile faded as he felt an odd draught *around his bottom.*

"Don't **look!**" gasped Fred. But of course Mouse *did*, and...

"My tail!" he wailed. "Why, why ... it's *gone*. But I LOVED my tail *so much!*"

OSH!

He marched up to Phoebe. "Put it *back!*"

"Absolutely not!" she replied.

Mouse stamped his foot. "Best of three then!" he cried. "We play two more games, and if I win *both*, I jolly well get my tail back!"

"**Not so fast, Mouse!**" gulped Fred. "What if you *lose?* You could end up like the *Barely Theres*."

But it was too late.

"Ha!" roared Phoebe, glaring at Mouse. "You're **ON!**"

Next they played **spin.** It was one of Phoebe's favourites.

"We each get *ten* toy flying saucers," she said. "And we make them spin on sticks. The one with the most spinning at the end of five minutes wins."

Fred was in charge of the timer. And the Barely Theres had to pass them the flying saucers.

"Ready, set – **GO!**" called Fred, and Phoebe got spinning right away.

She was good. And really fast. Then Mouse saw why. The height of their sticks was just right for *her*. But he had to reach up on tippy toes! Yet again, Phoebe Fairplay was NOT playing fair...

Soon Phoebe had nine flying saucers spinning, while Mouse only had four.

"Two minutes to go!" Fred shouted. Mouse was going to lose!

But as Captain Bushy passed Mouse a flying saucer, he whispered, "She's never done *ten*."

"Eh?" replied Mouse.

But suddenly he got it!

If he could persuade Phoebe to try and beat her record, all her flying saucers might tumble...

"Hey, Phoebe!" called Mouse. "You're doing, um ... ACES. But I wouldn't try to beat your record."

"I won't!" snapped Phoebe. "Though I *can* ... i-if I want. It's up to ME."

Mouse grinned as Phoebe snatched up one last flying saucer. A few of her nine were already wobbling, but she was too busy to notice.

"Thirty seconds left!" shouted Fred.

Phoebe quickly plonked the saucer on to a stick and sent it spinning – but it wobbled dangerously.

"Silly thing!" she muttered, whipping it off and starting it again.

Mouse glanced over. Her *other* nine were now teetering, while *his* four spun with ease!

Then...

CRASH! CRASH!

CRASH!

Phoebe's saucers came tumbling down.
"NO!" she roared.

"Time's up!" called Fred, almost cheering with relief. "And the winner of spin iiiiiiiiiiis ... **Mouse!**"

Mouse did a little victory dance wiggling his tail-less bottom.

"I win! I win! A cha-cha-cha. I win!"

Phoebe kicked a flying saucer.

"But I WON'T lose the last game. Meet me at the funfair in one hour. At the Intergalactic Highway – my roller coaster. We're having a race. You two against me. And you'll need something to race in."

"But we don't *have* anything," gasped Fred.

Phoebe shrugged. "That's your problem."

Turning to her chess set, she gave a shrill whistle and one of the horses reared up and trotted over.

Phoebe jumped on and galloped away.

"Oh!" she called back. "And don't be late!"

*

The roller coaster was awesome! It had loops and twirls and daring deep dips into darkness.

Phoebe was in a snazzy chariot drawn by all four horses from her chess set. Their hooves had been fitted with super-whizzy castors.

"Huh! We should be in *that*," grumbled Mouse as he and Fred squeaked up. "The shield that Wilbur gave us *goes* with that chariot." Their vehicle had been kindly loaned to them by the Barely Theres. It was the old broken rocket they'd crashed in long ago, and it was very rusty. But it *did* have a (sometimes) working light and a packet of mints in the glove compartment. Plus, they'd tied on pedals and wheels. *And* oiled them.

"A GO-KART? Pathetic!" Phoebe snorted as they positioned themselves on the track. Mouse and Fred had one pedal each.

"Ready, Mouse?" asked Fred. And Mouse gave a nod.

"I was born ready," he replied. "Plus, my bottom is *freezing* – I need my tail back!"

The littlest Barely There raised the starter flag in its invisible hand.

"R-ready..." it stuttered.

"Steady..." it gulped.

"Oh, for goodness' sake!" Phoebe flicked the reins and – "Yahhhhh!" – left Fred and Mouse for stardust!

"She's *cheating*," gasped Mouse. "Step on it, Ferret. GO!"

4

The old rocket hadn't gone so fast in LIGHT Years. The oil kicked in after a few dodgy bends then they really started picking up speed.

"Wheeee!" They looped the loops.

"Ahhh!" They dived the dips.

"Boom!" They burst through the stars.

But Phoebe was ahead at every turn.

"Faster!" yelled Mouse. "She cannot win. I look like a *guinea pig* without my tail!"

The wind certainly blew the cobwebs off

as they flew into the final tunnel, which was lit with huge crystals.

Phoebe was still ahead but they were gaining fast. As she neared the end of the tunnel she turned around and waved. A second later, the crystal lights went off.

"I can't see!" shrieked Fred.

"SHE did that!" yelled Mouse.

The rocket bounced off the walls as Fred struggled to steer in the dark.

"Hang on!" he cried. "And keep pedalling!" He felt around the dashboard until his paw found a switch and – ting! – their one small light flickered on.

"Phew!" they gasped. It was just enough to keep them on track.

"Come ON!" yelled Mouse as they shot from the tunnel. Phoebe was now close to the finish line.

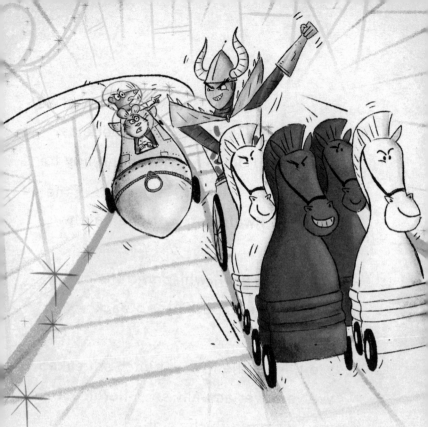

Mouse and Fred pedalled on, inching
closer as Phoebe's horses started to tire.
Then – by a whisker – over the finish line
went ... a rusty nose-cone!

"I – I mean we – did it!" cried Mouse.

Fred punched the air. "And now you'll get
your tail back! After all, it's only fair..."

"Stand STILL!" snapped Phoebe as Mouse dusted down his bottom, ready to receive his tail.

Fred stood watching with the Barely Theres.

"Her right horn," whispered the curly whiskers, "shoots out Putting Back Powder."

"We think," the littlest bunch squeaked.

"We've never actually seen her *use* it before," Captain Bushy sighed.

Fred nodded. He suddenly felt ever so sorry for the Barely Theres. They'd *never* win against Phoebe, so they'd never get their bodies back.

"Unless..." Fred muttered to himself. He'd just had a risky, but really rather great, idea!

As Phoebe's right horn found its target, Fred felt for Wilbur's *shield* in his backpack.

"Ready?" boomed Phoebe.

"Ready!" beamed Mouse, and...

¡WHOOSH!

The gush of purple powder that
shot from the horn hit Mouse
square on the bottom.

"My tail!" cried Mouse.
"I see it coming back!"

When it looked all
there, Fred thrust
the shield into
the bright purple
powder.

TING!

The powder ricocheted off it and
fountained into the air. As it floated back
down it landed on the Barely Theres.

"Ooooo!" Their whiskers curled into big
smiles as their bodies started to reappear.
They looked like sea lions. But *alien* ones
with spots and funny whiskers!

"Now **GO!**" hissed Fred, shooing them into Phoebe's chariot.

Mouse tossed them the mints from their old rocket. "To give your horses *energy*," he cried.

Then... **WHOOSH!** off they sped up the roller coaster, the funny little aliens cheering.

"And at the top," called Fred, "leave the track and burst through the jigsaw sky!"

"We will! We will!" all three called back. "And thank you!"

That just left Fred and Mouse to skedaddle. But Phoebe – who'd been gaping in disbelief – had found her voice again...

"How **DARE** you!" she bellowed. "No one outsmarts **ME.** You'll pay for this!"

She strode to the Jungle ride.

"**HUGSY!**" she roared, and a huge boa constrictor slithered out.

"Hug them!" demanded Phoebe. But it was too late. Fred had whisked Mouse into the rocket and off they pedalled up the track.

Up – up – and away they soared through the freshly made hole in the sky.

"Hold on to your tail, Mouse," chuckled Fred.

"To infinity and beyond!"

The
Coggles

To **infinity and beyond** was amazing. Even Mouse thought so.

They flew the old rocket at top speed, dodging comets and chasing shooting stars. When they finally touched down on a faraway planet, Mouse's eyes lit up.

"*Robots,*" he gasped, gazing around. They were everywhere, doing all kinds of jobs. Some were sweeping, some picking fruit, while others spruced up spaceships.

"Wow!" cried Fred. "And *look there...*"

They'd landed near a bank of whirring windmills made from scraps of metal. Their arms turned in the gentle breeze from the big black hole above.

"Now this is my kind of planet," said Mouse, hopping out of the rocket. "I *love* robots!"

"*Shh – someone's coming!*" whispered Fred as the door of a windmill creaked open.

Fred and Mouse watched as three space *caterpillars* came clip-clopping out. Their bodies were bright green, like strings of pom-poms. They had lots of hands, all waving brightly and many feet in big, clumpy boots.

"*Phew...*" whispered Fred, "they look friendly. No chance of you losing your tail *here*, Mouse!"

"Welcome to Planet Cog," said the biggest caterpillar, "home of the Coggles, and our inventions." His eyes twinkled behind half-moon spectacles. "I'm Fizzleworth Fixit and these are my grandchildren."

"I'm Clippa," said the girl.

"And I'm Clopp," said the boy. "Who are you?"

"Mouse," replied Mouse. "And this is ... Ferret."

"Mostly known as Fred," Fred explained.

Just then, a robot puppy came bounding out of the windmill, heading straight for Mouse.

"Ruff ruff! Cuckoo!"

"**Argggh!**" squealed Mouse.

"Don't be scared. He's just saying hello," said Clippa. "Grandpa made him from a broken old clock, which is why he *sometimes cuckoos.*"

"Grandpa's an amazing inventor," said Clopp.

"Why, thank you," Grandpa blushed.

"So am I!" nodded Mouse. "I'll have you know, I'm actually a BRILLIANT inventor."

"Of course you are!" Fred snorted under his breath.

"Well, it's lovely to meet you," said Grandpa Fixit. "Would you like to see more of our inventions?"

"We'd *love* to," cried Mouse eagerly.

They followed the Coggles inside the windmill. The big, round room was full of inventions.

A robot on shiny silver wheels whizzed up to Fred and helped him off with his backpack.

"Neat!" Fred gasped.

A mechanical arm then shot out of the wall and took off Mouse's helmet.

"Told you we like inventing things," said Clippa, grinning.

"And today is a very special day," added Grandpa. "It's our 'Build-a-Bot Showcase'."

"Your what case?" asked Mouse.

"Our SHOWcase!" beamed Clopp. "Every year we make robots from leftover bits, then show them off in the Showcase."

"A competition!" whooped Mouse, and Fred gave a groan. Mouse and competitions spelled TROUBLE.

"Mouse," he whispered. "No taking over."

"As if!" Mouse grinned back.

He turned to the children. "Can we see your robots?"

"Sure!" cried Clopp, and he and his sister hurried Fred and Mouse up lots of stairs to their attic workroom.

"I made a Skate-Bot Snail," said Clippa proudly. "As it roller-skates, it leaves a shiny trail!"

The Skate-Bot Snail was an old tin can with a big, curly shell glued on top.  Under the can was a row of ball bearings.

Clippa sent the snail whizzing, and from the back of the can came a glug of what looked like dirty bathwater.

"And I made a Burpy-Bot Bug," grinned Clopp, "from a growler out of an old teddy."

It had been painted to look like a spotty beetle, with a winder glued on to the side. Clopp wound it up and it started to jiggle. Then it let out a loud

BURP!

and fell over.

Mouse frowned. "Those aren't *robots*," he muttered. The children's faces fell.

"W-what Mouse means," said Fred hastily, "is those aren't ... *just* robots. They're BRILLIANT ones – eh, Mouse?"

Mouse shook his head. "But I could *make* them brilliant if I borrowed a couple of tools. Then they'd be sure to win the competition."

"Here it's not just about winning," replied Clopp. "Although," he added brightly, "Grandpa's robot is **bound** to win because it's **super-duper.**"

"Now *that* sounds more like it!" Mouse looked around.

"It's in the cellar," explained Clopp.

"And to see it," grinned Clippa, "you have to take the helter-skelter slide – and it's *awfully* fast..."

Mouse laughed.
"As if I'm scared of
an iddy-biddy slide.
Let's go! In fact,
I'll go FIRST."

2

"Arggghh!"

Mouse shot off the end of the slide and landed **BUMP!** on his bottom. A faint trickle of smoke wafted from his tail.

"No one said it was *that* fast," he grumbled, getting up.

He looked around. There were tools everywhere. Saws, hammers, screwdrivers and spanners dangled from hooks in neat rows. On the workbench were tubs full of nuts, bolts and cogs – and inventions lined the curved walls.

"Look at that one!"

Mouse raced over to a smart-looking robot as Fred bumped on to the floor, followed by Clippa and Clopp.

The robot was made of metal and looked a bit like a penguin. Its big, round tummy almost touched the floor, and its flat feet stuck out from under it. Instead of wings, it had arms, and a tuft of springy copper-coloured hair sprouted from its head.

"That's Simon," said Clippa. "He's Grandpa's entry for the Showcase."

"You mustn't touch," Clopp added quickly.

Mouse nodded back, thoughtfully eyeing up the tools.

"Simon's a Pamper-Bot," Clopp went on. "All the adults are making Pamper-Bots this year. They might cut hair. Or massage your feet. Simon does manicures – so he trims and files nails. He also paints them colours that change with your mood. It's so cool!"

Mouse, however, did not look impressed.

"He only does *nails*? What are all *those* for then?"

He pointed along the workbench to a box of inventions.

Clopp leaned over, and one of his many hands fished out a bright blue toothbrush.

"Gramps invented all kinds of pamper *add-ons*," he explained, "then chose the best ones. These weren't up to scratch."

Mouse strolled over and had a quick nosy inside the box.

"My favourite's the self-curling curlers," said Clippa. "There are back-scratching hairbrushes too."

Clopp jiggled the toothbrush and it started to whistle a tune.

"Huh!" Mouse shrugged. "I would add them *all*. The more the better – *if* you ask me."

"But they're *not* asking you," whispered Fred.

"Well, they *should* be," nodded Mouse, rolling up his sleeves. "I'm a dab hand with

robots. And this one needs a few small ...
'improvements'."

He snatched up a screwdriver. And
before they could blink, Mouse was taking
off Simon's tummy panel.

"*Wait!*" gulped Fred.

"*Noooooooooo!*" squealed the
children.

"Really, it's fine!" chuckled Mouse. "I'm
just putting your grandpa's add-ons from
that box ... into some secret compartments
I'm making."

"I d-don't think—" spluttered Clippa.

"Please stop—" spluttered Clopp as
Mouse measured and hammered away.

"With my secret compartments," he
chattered on, "no one will *even* know
they're there until *I* decide to whizz them
into action. Then Simon *WILL* win and—"

"**Mouse!**" hissed Fred. "*I insist—*"
But suddenly he stopped.

Mouse was neat and fast. And to Fred's amazement, he *did* seem to know what he was doing. The children saw too, and their panicked frowns were replaced with astonished grins.

"You're welcome!" beamed Mouse. He looked very smug. "At home I've got *medals* for inventing, you know. They fill the house!"

With his secret compartments done, Mouse grabbed the box of add-ons.

"Now before I hide these in the robot's tummy," he said, "I'll just improve them too!"

First, he made the self-curling curlers twirl faster. Then he gave the back-scratching hairbrushes more bristles.

Finally, he made
the toothbrush
sing a proper
song instead
of just whistling.

As Mouse popped them into their secret compartments, Clippa and Clopp beamed. But Fred was looking twitchy again...

"What if Simon runs out of steam?" he asked. "That's a *lot* of extra stuff you've added."

"I've already thought of that, thank you!" replied Mouse. "A tin of *oil*, see?"

He placed it into the final compartment.

"*That* should keep him going," nodded Mouse, popping Simon's tummy panel back in place.

"Hey, wait – that's Grandpa's soup..." said Clopp. "He snacks on it when he's working late at night."

"Nonsense!" snorted Mouse. "*That* is clearly OIL. If anyone should know the difference, it's ME – I am, after all (not wishing to boast) a robot-building genius!"

116

Next Mouse got to work on his *own* remote control.

"I'll use *this*," he explained, "when the time is right to make those hidden inventions spring to life. Then everyone will see what Simon can REALLY do!"

"Can't *we* see what he does now?" asked Fred. "Just to make sure it all … works."

"Oh, Ferret!" grinned Mouse. "You worry too much. But fine! Take a seat in

my 'Pamper Parlour' and prepare to be
AMAZED!"

Mouse arranged some stools and they all sat down. Then he picked up *Grandpa's* remote control.

"Right!" Mouse flicked a switch, and Simon whirred to life and gave them all a very neat manicure.

"Oooo!" Clippa's nails were all the colours of the rainbow. "That means my mood's bright," she said. Fred frowned. *His* nails were candy-floss pink. What did that mean?

Mouse then picked up *his* remote control. "Time for some *proper* pampering," he nodded.

He pressed a button and the self-curling curlers SPRANG out and gave everyone bouncy ringlets in their hair. Fred wasn't too sure, but Clippa and Clopp loved *their* curls.

Next, Mouse spun a little dial and the back-scratching hairbrushes scratched all along their backs.

"It tickles!" snorted Clopp in fits of giggles.

Finally, Mouse flicked a switch and the toothbrush got to work on Fred's teeth. As it did, it sang cheerily, '*The Sun Has Got His Hat On*'.

"I'm ACES at choosing songs," said Mouse, tapping along. "Much better than plain old whistling!"

But there was one more surprise up Mouse's sleeve. A little invention he'd added *of* his *own*.

He twiddled a lever and a hand on a spring twanged out of the robot's side clutching a *cleaning cloth*. As Simon began polishing everyone's boots, Fred couldn't believe his eyes.

"You know, Mouse," he said. "I was worried at first. But fair play, you've done a great job."

Mouse patted himself on the back

and took a bow.

"Clever me!"

Just then, Grandpa's voice echoed down the slide. "Time for the Showcase!"

"Coming!" called Clippa.

"We'll bring Simon up," called Clopp.

Mouse quickly popped the add-ons back into their hidey holes and closed the tummy compartment.

He slipped his remote control into his pocket. "And no telling!" he grinned. "It'll be a surprise. How EXCITING!"

✳

The biggest windmill on the planet was buzzing with Coggles and their very clever inventions.

"Wow!" gasped Fred and Mouse.

"Here nothing goes to waste..." explained Grandpa.

When the judge had inspected all the children's robots, Mouse hurried Fred to have a look.

The youngest children had made Pet-Bots, which were really fun. Clippa's Skate-Bot Snail had run out of bathwater, but Clopp's Burpy-Bot Bug was still making very rude noises.

Fred liked a knitting Hamster-Bot made from an old tennis ball and bendy levers.

BuRrRrRpPpP!

"And look at that toilet roll Owl-Bot!" cried Mouse. Its jam-jar-lid eyes spun round and round like Catherine wheels.

Next along were the Helper-Bots the older children had made. These whizzed around doing helpful jobs – like serving cakes and pouring milkshakes.

"Now *I* would have made them mop up the spills too!" sniffed Mouse.

Finally, the teenagers had made Spy-Bots that tracked your every move. Some even made you crack a code to get into the loo!

"Well done to all the children!" exclaimed the judge. And everyone got a medal and a clap.

"See, Mouse?" grinned Clippa. "Our robots were fine as they were!"

"I *still* could have made them better..." muttered Mouse.

It was time for the adults to show off their robots. And now there would only be *one* winner.

"All Pamper-Bots on to the stage!" called the judge, and Grandpa joined a long line of Coggles wheeling their robots into position.

Mouse and Fred took their seats in the audience beside Clippa and Clopp.

"Exciting eh, Ferret?" Mouse's eyes twinkled. "I can't wait to whip out *my* remote control. The judge will be blown away!"

"I hope so," whispered Fred.

Mouse gave a nod. "I KNOW so!"

One by one, the Pamper-Bots showed off their skills.

The first gave the judge a neat trim and blow dry.

"Not bad," sniffed Mouse. "But Simon's self-curling curlers will do better!"

The next robot along was a Style-Bot. A nifty conveyor belt spun around its tummy as it styled the judge with various bits and bobs.

"Ooops!" sniggered Mouse. "Sunglasses

with a *bobble hat*? WRONG!"

The third robot gave her a 'No-Mess Face Mask', which disappeared with a twinkly *poof!*

"Wow," gulped Fred, and even Mouse sat up.

"S-show off," he tutted nervously. "But Simon can beat *anything* thanks to me."

The judge continued along the line, finally stopping at Simon. Grandpa flicked the switch on his remote control and the robot gave her a relaxing hand massage, then painted her nails with *zero* drips.

"Sunshine yellow!" beamed Clippa. "That colour means she's happy."

"She'll be even happier," said Mouse, "when I show her what *else* he can do."

When the robots had all performed, the judge strolled along the line trying to decide on a winner. Mouse sat waiting, and the *second* she got to Simon, he pressed a button on *his* remote and...

TWANG!

the self-curling curlers shot out and gave her big, bouncy ringlets!

"Eh?" gasped Grandpa. But the judge seemed delighted.

"Oh my!"

With a satisfied nod, Mouse now spun a dial and...

DINK-A-DINK!

the back-scratching hairbrushes appeared and gently scratched the judge's back.

"Up a bit!" she giggled. "Down a bit! Left! Ahh – lovely!"

It was going so well. Until...

"Smoke!" whispered Fred. *"Mouse – LOOK! – around the robot's back!"*

The children had seen it too. "Oh no!" they gulped. Simon was overheating.

"Don't panic!" shrieked Mouse, jabbing random buttons. "Work you silly thing!"

DOINNNGGG!

All the add-ons started working at once, but NOT as they just had. The toothbrush was blowing raspberries as it brushed the judge's *glasses*. The hairbrushes were sword-fighting. And Simon was stuffing handfuls of curlers into the judge's handbag!

"**Good gracious,**" gasped Grandpa, completely befuddled.

"Mouse!" hissed Fred.

"**I'm fixing it!**" growled Mouse. He jabbed the remote extra hard but this just made things worse.

The tin of 'oil' now exploded from Simon's tummy all over the judge's boots.

"My pea and ham soup!" Grandpa scratched his head as a hand clutching a cloth twanged out of Simon's side and rubbed it in!

Grandpa looked at the audience with a baffled shrug.

"Time we made a move, Mouse," gulped Fred.

He whipped the party popper from his backpack and...

POP!

a storm of tickertape shot into the air.

While everyone was distracted, Fred found the toy rocket that Wilbur had given him in the shop.

"Grab hold of this
– NOW!" he
commanded Mouse.
And for once Mouse
did as he was told.

In a blur of
stars and a rush
of wind...

...they found themselves back in the Story Shop.

"Good adventure?" grinned Wilbur as he clutched Mouse's storybook.

"Only because I was so BRILLIANT," boasted Mouse, whipping the book from Wilbur's hand and flicking through the pages. "I hope you included my magnificent cooking skills and how ACES I am at handling *aliens*."

He marched to the door.

"Oh, and Ferret," he said. "No need to thank me for saving you – *countless times*." And off he went, tail in the air.

"Well, *he* was very big for his space boots!" chuckled Wilbur.

Fred grinned. "Nothing I couldn't handle."

"Time for tea?" asked Wilbur.

Fred's eyes twinkled. "Now that," he said, hanging up his backpack, "would definitely be **out of this world!**"

What kind of **Story Shop**
adventure would suit you?
Turn the page to find out!

The Story Shop Quiz

Question 1
You're allowed a pet. What's it to be?
a) A cat
b) A parrot
c) A lizard
d) A starfish

Question 2
You're feeling a bit peckish. What's your go-to snack?
a) Anything I can magic up
b) Fish fingers
c) A rock cake
d) A wedge of smelly cheese!

Question 3
It's the weekend! Would you rather...
a) Go walking in a dark wood
b) Hang out at the seaside
c) Visit the zoo
d) Take a trip to a planetarium

Question 4
Your friend comes over to play. Do you...
a) Make a potion

b) Go treasure hunting
c) Build a den
d) Play computer games

Question 5
You're having a nightmare! Would you rather...
a) Be turned into a frog
b) Walk the plank into shark-infested waters
c) Come face to face with the owner of some gigantic footprints
d) Be chased by little green aliens

Question 6
What's your favourite fairground ride?
a) Ghost train
b) River rapids
c) I prefer the adventure playground
d) The highest, fastest rollercoaster

Question 7
What would you most like to be when you grow up?
a) A scientist
b) Rich!
c) A paleontologist
d) An astronaut

Add up your answers to find your
perfect adventure!

Mostly As – An Abracadabra
Magical Adventure!
Saddle up your broomstick and grab
your spell book as you discover
your inner magic. Explore creepy
castles, bust ghosts and turn
teapots into toads. Then it's time
for a midnight snack or two.
Sandwitches, or finger rolls?
But beware ... wands can
have a mind of their own!

Mostly Bs – A Shiver-me-Timbers
Pirate Adventure!
Grab your cutlass and raise the Jolly Roger
because an adventure on the high seas is perfect
for you! Swab the deck, belt out sea shanties,
follow maps and dig for
buried treasure – a whole
chestful if you're lucky.
But beware ... you won't
be the only pirate after
that gold!

Mostly Cs – A Totally Roar-some Dinosaur Adventure!

Time to get into training for running FAST as a dinosaur adventure awaits you. Build hideouts, wash in rivers, light campfires with flint as you trek to find your prehistoric pals. But beware … don't tread on a T Rex's toes if you want to live to tell the tale!

Mostly Ds – An Out-of-this-World Space Adventure!

Pop on your space helmet and buckle up tight as you zoom off on a space trip of a lifetime! Travel where no human has gone before as you planet-hop through space meeting Martians, chasing comets and dodging shooting stars. But beware … not all aliens are friendly!

Tracey Corderoy is a multi-award winning author. Her first book was published in 2010 and she has since writtten over seventy books!

Her passion for nosing into other people's 'stories' began in early childhood, thanks to a set of encyclopaedias and a copy of *Cinderella*. Then one special teacher and many librarians fed Tracey more and more books. Between their pages real magic started to happen; books made her laugh, and cry and think. They made her feel that she could do things...

Tony Neal is a graphic artist and illustrator from South Leicestershire, England.

His passion for art and illustration has led him to a blooming career in children's book illustration where he now creates works for various publishing houses and clients worldwide. He has illustrated books for Usborne, Little Tiger Press, Simon & Schuster, Hachette Children's to name but a few. Tony's work is inspired by everyday life and the quirky details that surround us.

Look out for the
next **Story Shop**
adventure coming soon...

Pirates Ahoy!